Dear Parent:
Your child's love of re

MW01033269

Every child learns to read in a different way and at his or her own speed. You can help your young reader improve and become more confident by encouraging his or her own interests and abilities. You can also guide your child's spiritual development by reading stories with biblical values and Bible stories, like I Can Read! books published by Zonderkidz. From books your child reads with you to the first books he or she reads alone, there are I Can Read! books for every stage of reading:

SHARED READING
Basic language, word repetition, and whimsical illustrations, ideal for sharing with your emergent reader.

BEGINNING READING
Short sentences, familiar words, and simple concepts for children eager to read on their own.

READING WITH HELP
Engaging stories, longer sentences, and language play for developing readers.

READING ALONE
Complex plots, challenging vocabulary, and high-interest topics for the independent reader.

ADVANCED READING
Short paragraphs, chapters, and exciting themes for the perfect bridge to chapter books.

I Can Read! books have introduced children to the joy of reading since 1957. Featuring award-winning authors and illustrators and a fabulous cast of beloved characters, I Can Read! books set the standard for beginning readers.

A lifetime of discovery begins with the magical words **"I Can Read!"**

Visit www.icanread.com for information on enriching your child's reading experience.
Visit www.zonderkidz.com for more Zonderkidz I Can Read! titles.

[Jesus said], "I tell you ... there is joy in heaven
over one sinner who turns away from sin."
—Luke 15:10

Mrs. Rosey Posey and the Yum-Yummy Birthday Cake
Text copyright © 2008 by Robin's Ink, LLC
Illustrations copyright © 2008 by Christina Schofield

Requests for information should be addressed to:
Zonderkidz, Grand Rapids, Michigan 49530

Library of Congress Cataloging-in-Publication Data

Gunn, Robin Jones, 1955-
    Mrs. Rosey Posey and the yum-yummy birthday cake / story by Robin Jones Gunn ;
    pictures by Christina Schofield.
        p. cm. -- (I can read! Level 2)
    Summary: On her birthday, Mrs. Rosey Posey bakes a very special layer cake to share
    with her neighborhood friends, but when disaster strikes she shares a lesson about
    repentance, too.
    ISBN-13: 978-0-310-71579-5 (softcover)
    ISBN-10: 0-310-71579-2 (softcover)
    [1. Birthdays--Fiction. 2. Cake--Fiction. 3. Repentance--Fiction. 4. Conduct of life--
    Fiction. 5. Christian life--Fiction.] I. Schofield, Christina (Christina Diane), 1972- ill. II. Title.
PZ7.G972Mry 2008
E--dc22   2007034323

Editor: Betsy Flikkema
Art Direction: Jody Langley
Cover Design: Sarah Molegraaf

Printed in Hong Kong
08 09 10 11 • 4 3 2 1

ZONDERkidz | I Can Read! | 2 READING WITH HELP

Mrs. Rosey Posey
and the
Yum-Yummy
Birthday Cake

story by Robin Jones Gunn

pictures by Christina Schofield

Right in the middle of Poppyville

at the end of Merry Lane

is a big yellow house.

Mrs. Rosey Posey lives here.

Children love Mrs. Rosey Posey.

Poppyville

4

One sunny day,

Mrs. Rosey Posey got up early.

She said, "Today is my birthday.

I'm going to make a cake.

It will be yum-yummy."

Mrs. Rosey Posey baked all morning.

The first layer was chocolate

with peanut butter balls.

The next layer was strawberry.

The third layer was vanilla

with chunks of big fat brownies.

Was Mrs. Rosey Posey done yet?

Oh no. Next came kiwi and bananas.

Layer five was fudge with nuts.

Then came her favorite layer,

coconut cake with candy hearts.

Mrs. Rosey Posey smiled.

"I'll add an apple to the top,"

said Mrs. Rosey Posey.

This apple was dipped in caramel.

It was rolled in chocolate chips.

Every layer of the cake was perfect.

She carried the cake outside.

The birds were singing.

Mrs. Rosey Posey sang along.

She waited for the children to come.

Sarah and Sam came first.

"Hooray!" said Mrs. Rosey Posey.

"I am so glad you are here."

"What a beautiful cake!" said Sarah.

"Indeed," said Mrs. Rosey Posey.

"But you may not eat it yet."

14

"Then come with us," said Sam.

"We have a surprise," said Sarah.

The children led Mrs. Rosey Posey

to the front yard.

She opened her eyes.

It was a parade!

All her friends cheered and sang.

"Hooray for Mrs. Rosey Posey!"

They all marched down Merry Lane.

Sarah wanted to ride her bike

in the parade.

She ran back to get her bike.

The cake looked so yummy.

What do you think she did?

Sarah reached up, up, up.

She wanted to taste one chip

from the apple on the very top.

But Sarah bumped the table.

Suddenly, the cake began to wobble.

And then it happened.

KER-SPLAT!

The yum-yummy cake fell down.

"Oh no! Oh no! Oh no!" said Sarah.

She looked around. She was afraid.

She hid behind the porch.

Soon Mrs. Rosey Posey came.

She called, "Sarah? Sarah?

Where are you?"

"Here I am," said a small voice.

"Why are you hiding?"

asked Mrs. Rosey Posey.

"I wanted to taste the cake,"

said Sarah. "But I made it fall."

Mrs. Rosey Posey looked very sad.

Sarah began to cry. "I am so sorry."

"I know you are. I forgive you,"

said Mrs. Rosey Posey.

Sarah asked a wobbly question.

"Am I still special to you?"

"Oh yes," said Mrs. Rosey Posey.

She smiled at Sarah.

Her eyes had a twinkle.

Her smile had a zing.

Mrs. Rosey Posey had a secret.

"Sarah, did you know that
every time a person repents,
God has a big party in heaven?"

"What does repent mean?"
asked Sarah.
"Repent means saying you're
sorry and meaning it.
This makes God happy."

BIRTHDAY!

29

Sarah smiled.

Mrs. Rosey Posey said, "Do you know what makes me happy?"

"What?" asked Sarah.

"I like eating cake with my hands,"
said Mrs. Rosey Posey.
All the children did the same.
It was the yum-yummiest cake ever.

"Will you always be my friend, even if you don't like what I do?" Sarah asked Mrs. Rosey Posey. "Yes," she answered, "even then."